THE TABLETS I-XV

By Armand Schwerner

The Lightfall (1963)
The Domesday Dictionary (1964)
(if personal) (1968)
The Tablets I-VIII (1968)
Seaweed (1969)

THE
TABLETS
I-XV

Presented by the scholar-translator

Transmitted through

ARMAND SCHWERNER

Grossman Publishers, New York, 1971

The author wishes to express his gratitude to both
the City University and the State University
of New York for their helpful grants.

THE EMPTYING

KEY:
. . . . *untranslatable;*
+ + + + + + + *missing;*
(?) *variant reading;*
[   ] *supplied by the scholar-translator.*

TABLET I

All that's left is pattern* (shoes?).

> * doubtful reconstruction

I rooted about ... like a .... sow* for her pleasure

> * atavism: a hieroglyph; perhaps 'a fetal pig,' 'a small pig,' 'goddess'

the (power?) * for all of [us]!

> * perhaps 'damage,' if a borrowing; cf. cognate in N. Akkadian: 'skin-burn'

I made a mistake. The small path was barely muddy. Little squash;
and wet socks.* It is (scholarship?) (meditation?)

> * modernism. Specificity of attire a problem. Possibly 'underwear' (dryness?)

and the .... (energy?) the (energy?) the (pig?) * of the [mistake]!.....
(energy?)........

> * hieroglyph again: 'god' may be meant here

war/good-ness..../cunt* (thresher?)/marvel/cunt */bright-yellow/
bright-ochre†/bright-bright-yellow/bright-ochre-yellow/
bright-yellow-yellow-yellow-ochre-yellow‡§

> * hieroglyph, probably not syllabic. Very old 🐝: conceivably haloed by hair—but rake-like, very much the rake in the Kap-Kol-Bak-Silpotli-Wap frieze in the young consort's left hand. (See Ouspenskaya: *The Young Consort and the Rake Muckery*, Egypt. Annals, Surah P, P, iii.)
> † see Halevy-Cohen, *The Prismatic Function in Early Man: a study in Imperceptible Gradations*, U. U. Press, Ak., 1922–1962
> ‡ analogue of segmented compass readings? as NE, NNE, etc. We know the god Pri-Prik usually assumed yellow guises in his search for the eighteen-fold path. See Marduk, *The Babylonians*, Hirsute VII, Liber A–413, Tigris.

the emptying of yellow

\+ + + + + + + + + + +
\+ + + + + + + + + + + + + + +
\+ + + + +
\+ + + + +
\+ + + + +
he calls himself 'with grey horses'
he is 'having fine green oxen'
with (purpose?) + + + + + + + + + + + in the dream (nightmare?)
\+ + + + + + + + + + + + + + + of a sharp blade
[testicles] . . . . for the ground
shit (sweat?) upon the . . . .
rain upon the . . . .
saliva upon the . . . .
heart's blood upon the . . . .
children's strange (beautiful?) early blood in the . . . .
. . . . from the old dryness (underwear?)
vomit (yellow?/north?) does not slake ground
pus (ochre?/NNE?) does not stanch the wounds in the ground
bile (yellow-ochre?/NNNE?) does not + + + + + + + + +
he is splayed on the . . . . like a worn-out pig (god?)
he is un- + + + + + + + +
he is dis- + + + + + + + + + + +
he is + + + + + + + + + + + -less
he is de- + + + + + + + + + + +
he is impossible on the dry ground + + + + + + + + + before . . . .
he is non- + + + + + + + +
he is pre- + + + + + + + + + + +*

* the isolated prefix remnants are curious. The tablet seems rubbed out with care. Is this segment an early attempt to unite form and meaning? graphic as well as substantial emptiness?

the ants look (scrounge?) for food
the ground-pig (lower god?) sucks dry filth for water
the palaces are yellow (vomit?/N?)
look at the fishermen in their patterns (shoes?)!
they count the directions of emptiness by fish-names
N shad
E cod
S mackerel
W tuna
from the shad no rain weighs on the breeze
from the cod the loud wind is dry (unforgiving?) *

    * interesting. We find ourselves at or near the very
point in time where the word, concrete in origin,
shades off into an abstraction.

hanging-mackerel-tail-up-smoke-death*

    * virtually untranslatable. This is an attempt at an
Indo European nominalization of *kili-pap-swad-ur
plonz*. We can convey little of the conceptual cate-
gory 'fish-death,' rather 'up-down-fish-dying-becoming'
which refers in a coterminous visionary metaphysic to
both time-bound organisms (like the urus, say) and
the Death God, *plonz*, in his timeless brooding.

the tuna is mighty the tuna is mighty the way of up-down, smoke-death
the men dance around the stone
the stones dance over the pit
the pits dance beyond the bodies like the air-hog (god of low rain clouds?)
the bodies the bodies the bodies the bodies the bodies the bodies
beyond the bodies the trees dance
the bodies need to fuck the trees
the dry (unforgiving?) bodies wait twenty-eight days
the blood of the four bodies shad
the blood of the four bodies cod
the blood of the four bodies mackerel
the blood of the four bodies tuna*

    * four bodies here; six of them in the previous men-
tion. Odd.

they will change the bile
they will change the cold pus unless . . . . . . because . . . . fish-death
they will-would-might-have-can-change* the winter of NNE

> *tense untranslatable; outside Indo-European categories

do they destroy the ochre, the shad/shad-cod? do they eat?
they wait for the fat pig (god?)
+ + + + + + + + + +
+ + + + + + + + + + + +
+ + + + + + + + +
+ + + + + + + + + + + + + + + + +
+ + + + + +
+ + + + + + + +
+ +
. . . . of the great Ones (One?) *

> *capitalization clearly indicated. The number is in doubt. Is this the pig, or an incredible presage of the early Elohim?

+ + + + + + + +
+ + + + + + + + + + + +
+ + + + + + + + + + pattern (shoes?) . . . .
+ + + + + + + + + +
+ + + + + +
+ + + + + + + + + + + + +
+ + + + + + + + + ...

TABLET II

This tablet consists of a numbered list. At least a few of the units may be titles to chants which have never been found, or which may never have been written. Its exact placement in the context of the series is a problem.

1. empty holes in the fish-dying-becoming directions
2. . . . . strings and pieces + + + + + + + +
3. the children dance* in waters of fish-death

> * the idiosyncratic placement of the central horizontal cuneiform wedges suggests the word may be 'breathe.'

4. they are dry scales + + + + + + + + + + + + + +
5. on the inside their scales are wet (moist?)
6. they are empty holes; why do they walk and walk?
7. the + + + + + + + children eat. . . . . strings and pieces
8. the empty children run in [their] patterns (shoes?)
9. the pig (god?) waits . . . . fish-death
10. the children . . . .
11. the children . . . . ball games
12. the children . . . .
13. . . . . must eat (might-could-will-want-to-eat?) rain pintrpnit*

> * transliteration. Probably an archaic form of "alleluiah' or 'selah.'

14. the road . . . . penis-thinking pintrpnit
15. sometimes they walk on the river-road with crocodile pintrpnit
16. they can walk near the knom* in their stupid ignorance of fish-death

> * conceivably 'the Spirit which denies'

17. o they are stupid they are lacking they walk and walk
18. they separate fish and death
19. they do not separate fish and death
20. near the knom they tame the auroch pintrpnit
21. not far from the knom, on spring nights, they tame the urus pintrpnit
22. in stupid ignorance in stupid ignorance how do they walk and walk?
23. in walking the river road they tame wisent* pintrpnit

24. they are taller than urus pintrpnit
25. how small they are beside the urus pintrpnit
26. the . . . . to suck the rain
27. . . . . very warm on our knees
28. the long men* + + + + + + + + + + + + to eat the children

* possibly 'priests'

29. not merely to eat, but the blood . . . .
30. not merely to eat, but the knom . . . .
31. + + + + + + + + + + + + + + + + + forever
32. brains and liver . . . . many favors
33. the sun/the sun/the sun/the (power?)* for all of [us]!

* possibly 'damage'

34. we have made no mistake/the (energy?)/the (energy?)
35. the sun sits in the [testicles] of the pig (god?)
36. the sun +
37. the long house + + + + + + + yellow (N?/shad?/vomit?)
38. the sun from the cod
39. the sun from the cod
40. the sun from the cod
41. the sun from the cod
42. the sun from the cod pintrpnit

TABLET III

the further emptying

the calyx, the calyx, someone has ripped it
it will not make loam, it will crumble
the pig (god?) has pulled life off + + + + + + +
the pig (god?) is stronger than a thoughtless child
my chest empties .... my chest
I can no longer stand in the middle of the field and + + + + + + + +
I am missing, my chest has no food for the maggots
there is no place for the pollen, there is only a hole in the flower
the hummingbird .... pus .... nectar
the field is a hole without pattern (shoes?)
there are no eyes in the back of the wisent's sockets
the urus eats her own teats and her ....
the urus lies in milk and blood
the urus is a hole in the middle of the field
[testicles] .... for the ground
'with grey horses' drinks urine
'having fine green oxen' looks for salt
let us hold .... the long man upside down
let us look into his mouth .... selfish saliva
let us pluck + + + + + + + + + + + + + for brother tree
let us kiss the long man, let us carry the long man
let us kiss the long man, let us fondle the long man
let us carry the long man as the ground sucks his drippings
let us feel the drippings from his open groin
let us kiss the hot wound, the wet wound .... nectar
let us wait until he is white and dry .... my chest
let us look into his dry evil mouth, let us fondle the long man
let us bypass the wisent on the river-road pintrpnit
let us avoid the urus on the river-road pintrpnit
let us smell the auroch on the river-road pintrpnit
let us carry the beautiful (strange?) children to the knom
let us sing with the children by the knom

let us set the children's beautiful (strange?) skulls by the hearth
when the rain comes.
let us have rain
let us have rain
+ + + + + + + +
+ + + + + + + + + +
+ + + + ... tremble
and also to make the strangers piss in their pants for fear
and to make all neighbors know of the terrible . . . . . that is ours
let them hear about it, let them know
let them tremble like a spear going through the heart and through the back
let them become a knowing spear, let them bore in, fish-death
let them shake from the spear's blow, let them hear it sing
I need to feel my solid arm, I need to feel my mighty penis
o my son at the other edge of fish-death
o my son by the dark river-road I can't reach your fingertips
o my son in the rain your liver will make the barley shoot up
o my son in the rain your eyes will see the way in the wheat
o my son on the happy edge of the emptying, fish-death, pintrpnit
o dark dark dark dark dark dark dark dark dark dark
o dark
you will-would-might-have-can, let us have rain

TABLET IV

Most large fragments are the result of horizontal breaks. This Tablet (IV) and the next (V), however, are vertically fractured. The reconstruction of V is almost certainly correct. Doubt lingers about IV. The edges do not meet in three places; otherwise it is a good tight fit. Whether the idiosyncratic continuity derives from accident or design is a problem which only time and further studies and excavations will resolve. Note the cesuras.

is the man a bush on fire?
    like one drop of quartz, two cold onyx beads
is the man four-legged and with
               teeth?
    like one piece of petrified wood
is the man a hot woman?
    like one hard-finger-bone, one moonlight on iron
is he mud, of solid mud?
    in the shape of one clay tablet in frost
is the man a bird?
    . . . . like bronze eyes
is the unhappy man on all fours?
    in the shape of bronze statues of something wood
is the man all blood, all bile?
    like menstrual blood congealed in cold mud
is the woman a fat belly?
    like the world, a five-year-old's bloody . . .
is the man sleeping in a god?
    like a frog stuffed with small white stones
is the man's head aching?
    like . . . . . . empty + + + + + maggots
does the man play with her lips?
    like amber + + + + + + + running pus
can the man make himself come?
    like a . . . . cold onyx beads
can the woman come on top of the man?
    . . . . dead trees
when does the man sacrifice his hands?
    like sheep draped in cold mud
does the man wipe her belly with sperm?
    like stories about ice, about frozen
             wheat

does the man put good leaves under his
             testicles?
    + + + + + + + + + of maggots
does the man put his lips on the sheep's
             udder?
    in the shape of a clay tablet in frost
does the man put hand and elbow in his
             cow's vagina?
    like death in blossoms when . . . . .
does he ram his penis into soft earth?
    like the death in petrified wood
does he touch his woman's . . . . ?
    like the death in two cold onyx beads
does the man pray to her vulva for rain?
    like stories about ice, about frozen
             wheat

let's sacrifice this twig
let's sacrifice this great melon
let's sacrifice this shank
the hand is furious
the aching head screams
the sick groin is furious
+ + + + + + + + +
+ + + + + + + +
+ + + + + + + + + + +

what a pleasure!
what a pleasure!
what a terrific pleasure!
how will we frighten the strangers now?
how will they piss in their pants?
how will we frighten the strangers now?
+ + + + + + + + + +
+ + + + + + + + + + + + +
+ + + + + + + for water

TABLET VI

Here the scholar-translator has tried to approximate the colloquial tone of the original. Unfortunately we have no information about the identity of the addressee; anger and ridicule are directed toward some immanent power which keeps changing its attributes; rough approximations of its being may be embodied in variously found names: Big Fat Flux   Great Hole in the Cock Liver (perhaps a reference to poorly understood onanistic ritual practices directed to the air-hog or the ground-pig) Sore-Ass-Mole-Face-Snivel-Kra   Little Mover   Big Mover   Seventeen-Eyeball-Fusion-Up-Up   The One of This Way   The One of That Way   The One of No Way   Anxious-Liar-Fart-Flyaway The Smeller   The Digger   The Scheming Pintrpnit   The Porous Poppycock   The Mean-Sucking-Sponge-Pinipnipni   Pnouk   Lak   Pa-Pa-the-Flying-Slime   The Big Eater   The Paramount Groin of the Sucking Air   Old No-Name   The Rock   The Fly   The Killer of Water   The Beautiful (Strange?) Liar   The Rain-Spoiler   The Water Dryer   The Tree Dryer   The Flower Dryer The Urus Dryer   The Creep   The Knom of Lies The Great Trouble   The Scheming Rock   The Maggot   The Friendly Buzzard   Everybody's Hyena   The Dumpy Snivel   The Filthy Teat   The Foosh. It has been suggested that the concrete figures belong to an earlier layer; our knowledge, however, is not at such a point of sophistication that we can now attempt a Higher Criticism of this material. When we can, what germinative cultural possibilities might we not discover?

.... in the world. I can't come
you have oozed into my + + + + + + + + + old Water Dryer
 + + + + + + + + because when I reach the end of my story, I'll still have
all of it to tell in me waiting to explode
like the constipation in a plugged-up man after ....
Big Mover I still can't come, my woman is unhappy with me
she waits but she's getting + + + + + + + + and madder
old Water Dryer you are fat tree-gum and ...... and fungus in my loins
this is not me, o Pa-Pa-the-Flying-Slime, this is not me

I am not what I was, even my children know,
their jokes cover their pity, stories
about ice, about frozen wheat
show yourself Pnou, let me see you Lak,
come into my house with a face just once old No-Name
I will call you simple death
show yourself Lak, let me blind you Pnou
o Pinitou Pinitou Pinitou*, this is not me

* curious; if this is the surname, or given name, of the
speaker, we are faced for the first time with a particu-
larized man, *this* man, rescued from the prototypical
and generalized 'I' of these Tablets. If it is *this* man,
Pinitou, I find myself deeply moved at this early
reality of self; if we have here the name of an un-
known deity or peer of the speaker, I am not deeply
moved.

you are rainbow are you rainbow, I will hate it
if you are beautiful, Knom of Lies
Creep, Paramount Groin of the Sucking Air
· · · · · · · · · · · · · · · · · · [Great Hole] in the Cock Liver
knock in breaking + + + + + + + + + stone flames Killer of Water
Dumpy Snivel child-eye [sucker] faultfinder dry earth
dry breaking . . . . of a fault and another and two and three
· · child-eye Killer of Water
Mean-Sucking-Sponge-Pinipnipni . . . . and I
o Pinitou Pinitou Pinitou in dry cricket sperm
[break unhappy] my mouth is full of blood Beautiful (Strange?) Liar
I ate in a dream, I won + + + + + + + + + +, in a dream
you came to me Friendly Buzzard and took my
flow of a knocking to break me for the sucking you need
come see me when I . . . . I will call you
simple death, let me blind you Pnou
and [hide from] me then, steal away from me, I will
  + + + + + + + you Pa-Pa-the-Flying-Slime, I will
enclose you with sharp . . . . The Fly, I will
rake you with + + + + + + + + + + Filthy Teat, I will
  + + + + + + + + + + + + + + + + for Pinitou for Pinitou
who knows me I know me this is not me

I will + + + + + + + + + + + + face just once for my breaking mouth
I ate a Dumpy Snivel for a child-eye fault
[o my son by the dark] river-road I can't touch your fingertips
it was not me by the Knom who left you there
Friendly Buzzard please let me touch you
and tear your . . . ., please come into the . . . .
I will fondle you, I will open you up and eat your + + + + + + +
knock in breaking + + + + + + + + + + flames Killer of Water
+ +
+ + + + + + + + + flow + + + + + + + + + + +
. . . . The One of No Way . . . . unhappy with me
+ in the world, this place

TABLET VII

Unfortunately most of the following Tablet cannot be rendered into English. It has never been recovered. The original, which later disappeared, somehow passed into the hands of a certain Henrik L., an archaeologically gifted Norwegian divine. How he, working alone in the semi-darkness of late 19th century archaeology, managed to make anything at all of the text is itself a surpassing wonder. Even more taxing to common sense is his idiosyncratic translation method.

We know only that Henrik L. lived for three and a half years in Iceland, where he pursued his antiquarian researches. It was in this spirit that he approached his cuneiform Tablet, which he then translated into Crypto-Icelandic, a language we cannot yet understand. Only two segments of this extraordinary specialized version are clear; written in classical Old Icelandic, they probably derive from the skaldic *Völuspá*, the Prophecy of Völva, i.e. Witch or Seeress, written about 1,000 A.D.: 1. Vituð er enn eð hvat (Do you know now, or don't you?) 2. Festr mun stilna/ok freki rinna (The chain will break/the wolf will get out). In addition, the phrase 'faigðar orð' probably means 'word of doom.' The sequence 'feigðar orð' does appear in Old Icelandic material. The substance of this Tablet, insofar as intuition and scholarship can make out, certainly belongs in the context of this series, The Emptying. To complicate matters further, Henrik L. adds another symbol to the standard list used in editing the ancient Mesopotamian texts. Together with such signs as .... (untranslatable), + + + + + (missing), [ ] (supplied by the scholar-translator), and so on, he includes also ⊕ ⊕ ⊕ ⊕ ⊕, which he explains to mean 'confusing.' Tablet VII appears to be a nightmare-poem of dissolution, edged with faint hopes of ultimate rebirth.

The reader will notice one further odd intercalation, the old pastor's interjection of another anachronism, in this case Lutheran religious material, into the body of this Tablet. His devoutness ran away with his archaeological fidelity. On balance however we are lucky to have this beautifully musical text. Was it T. S. Eliot who wrote that he could listen by the hour to poetry in languages foreign to him, with delight in the rhythm and in the sound?

rötete rötete rötete þropörpe nok pintrpnöte
⊕ ⊕ ⊕ ⊕ ⊕ ⊕ ⊕ ⊕ ⊕ ⊕ ⊕ ⊕ ⊕ ⊕ + + + + + +

+ + + + + + + + + + + + + ... ⊕ ⊕ ⊕ ⊕ ⊕
⊕ ⊕ ⊕ ⊕ ⊕ ⊕ ⊕ ⊕ + + + + + + + ⊕ ⊕ ⊕ ⊕ ⊕ ⊕
⊕ ⊕ ⊕ ⊕ ⊕ ⊕ ⊕ ⊕ ⊕ ⊕ ⊕ ⊕ ⊕ ⊕ ⊕

⊕ ⊕ ⊕ ⊕ ⊕ ⊕ ⊕ ⊕ . . . . + + + + + freki
+ + + + ... + + + + + + + + + + +
+ + + + + + + ... ⊕ ⊕ ⊕ ⊕ ⊕ . . . . + + + +
⊕ ⊕ ⊕ ⊕ ⊕ ⊕ ⊕ ⊕ ⊕ ⊕ ⊕ ⊕ ⊕ ⊕ ⊕ ⊕ ⊕ ⊕ ⊕
. . . . + + + + + + + + + + + + ⊕
hraldar gronen panaknómen gardú
etaión pnaupnau gott Jesu Kriste

vituð ér enn eð hvat?

þögn of gat hroirðúk papapa
. . . . [faigðar orð]
rötete rötete rötete Jesu Kriste sakrifise
þorgilson þranódon hvat hvat papa
leggi steypðir pintrpnöte
folklass þanns punka hworis
+ + + + + + + + + + + + + + + punka hworis
⊕ ⊕ ⊕ ⊕ ⊕ ⊕ ⊕ ⊕ ⊕ ⊕ ⊕ ⊕ ⊕ ⊕ ⊕ punka hworis

vituð ér enn eð hvat?
festr mun stilna/ok freki rinna

hraldar gronen Jesu Kriste sacrifise þranódon
þögn gardú etaión nok þök
panaknómen proþörpe pintrpnöte ak Pinitu

vituð ér enn eð hvat?
festr mun stilna/ok freki rinna

(28 lines + + + + + + + + + + + + + + + + + + +)

ok freki ok freki ok freki ok freki ok freki

TABLET VIII

go into all the places you're frightened of
and forget why you came, like the dead

what should I look for?
what should I do? where?
aside from you, great Foosh,
who is my friend? a little stone,
a lot of dirt, a terrible headache
and more than enough worry about my grave. Hogs
will swill and shit on me, men
will abuse me

take your wedges and your mallet
wipe the sand from the stone, wipe the stone
clean of dead worms and bugs and waste
keep things clean

what am I supposed to do then?

the right words wait in the stone
they'll discover themselves as you chip away,
work faster, don't think as long as you want,
like men who wait

all right here's what I found
what a rush at the last minute
what a cold place, I'm thirsty
this curse better work;
here it is, but
what a cold place
to work fast in
I'm getting stiff, this curse
better work:

if you step on me
may your leg become green and gangrenous
and may its heavy flow of filth
stop up your eyes forever, may your face
go to crystal, may your meat be glass
in your throat and your fucking
fail. If you lift your arms in grief
may they never come down and you be known
as Idiot Tree and may you never die

if you pick your nose on my grave
may you be fixed forever in a stupid
attitude, may the children use you
as a jungle gym and turn your muscles to piss,
may you never find a place to sit
and your backbone tire beyond relief,
wherever you stumble around may your heavy feet
squish urus dung and you smell like plague
and you be known
as Fool and Loser and may you never die

if you throw your garbage on my grave
may its spirit haunt you and sneak into your bed
may your skin become viscous
from the visits of grease, may your woman
become bright with loathing
and sneer at your balls. May your nostrils
be stuffed with the spirit of garbage
and you be known as Big Nose and Fat Head
and may you never die

if you pass my grave and ignore
intruders you hear, may your ears
grow hammers and the mouse's squeak
crash like boulders on boulders and birdsong
shriek without end and the rustle

of high grass cut you like a scythe
and may you never become deaf and be known
as Coward and Alone
and may you never die

whoever drinks in this spirit of Ending
comes at last to these frightening places
and finds rock for his mallet . . . .
. . . .
. . . . to find words like lined leaves
but unlike the lined leaves they have me
memorable. What I leave adds me to you. It is
another place. Talk on the stone moves
for you, like boats on a bay, like cuts on bark,
like tracks on stone snow, like iron urus
on winter clay, like iron urus, pintrpnit!
When I'm wound around with wax, say so
on stone. I leave my mallet, pintrpnit!
I can still turn any way, touch my thigh, feel
the heavy trees whose birds go down,
I tower above the grass. It will not grow
forever but thank you thank you that I can chip
all this Ending like tracks on stone snow,
thank you, pintrpnit! + + + + + + + + + + + + + + +
+ the hardest seed.

. . . .
. . . .
. . . . to take him into that place and shroud him in wax
embellished with leaves. And as they did they joked and jeered for Pnou
and laughed for Lak. The long men humped young girls
and sang for the Tree Dryer. Too much food and they vomited
for the Big Mover. What the boys bore to the Knom! How
the women danced around the famished bull!
The long men skinned a rabbit live
for the Mean-Sucking-Sponge-Pinipnipni: take it,
grab it, play, flay it again, leave us alone, we are
waxing Pinitou

The reader who has followed the course of these Tablets to this point may find, upon looking back to Tablet 1 particularly, that I have been responsible for occasional jocose invention rather than strict archaeological findings. I now regret my earlier flippancy—an attitude characteristic of beginnings, a manifestation of the resistance a man often senses when he faces the probability of a terrific demand upon his life energy. Looking back myself to that first terrific meeting with these ancient poems, I can still sense the desire to keep them to myself all the while I was straining to produce these translations —desperately pushing to make available what I so wanted to keep secret and inviolable.

In addition I am worried that I may have mistranslated part of the preceding Tablet, a combination of dialogue and narrative. How unsteady the ground I am plowing, walking on, measuring, trying to get the measure of.... There is a growing ambiguity in this work of mine, but I'm not sure where it lies. Some days I do not doubt that the ambiguity is inherent in the language of the Tablets themselves; at other times I worry myself sick over the possibility that *I* am the variable giving rise to ambiguities. Do I take advantage of the present unsure state of scholarly expertise? On occasion it almost seems to me as if I am inventing this sequence, and such a fantasy sucks me into an abyss of almost irretrievable depression, from which only forced and unpleasurable exercises in linguistic analysis rescue me.

TABLET IX

because the terror they* afflict me with is well-known

* The Foosh? Old No-Name? The Fly? The Creep?

. . . . .the fire which is palsy. .penis
because the raaling the goruck me lightthring paws ship

+ +
and what will you do when your words give out
when the dumb whose blood is paste in a hot mouth
. . . . + + + + + + + + + + + + + + + + + purple foxglove*

* one of the first mentions of the finger shaped plant,
source of digitalis, the heart stimulant; intense con-
sciousness? rise into awareness?

because the paste lightthring paws ship
because repulsives in sperm-offerings dry in a big cockshead box pintrpnit
because the sinuous fever snakes through my bone-ends makes me crazy
reminds my body of sacrifice, they follow they afflict they follow
and what will I do when my glue words dry and lightthring dust paws ship
they is *you* and *anyone*, dust sperm and a crush of mush brains pity
because the dumb follow in slow death the riven owl Old No-Name
and cry soundlessly like cut wheat and can only live shrinking
. . . . + + + + + + + + + + + + + + + + + and yesterday
the fresh waters teemed with upturned lips of jelly
with tentacles and the tiny mouth
and yesterday the fresh waters teemed
with the fat upside-down jelly mouth trailing forests*

* touching instance of close zoological observations:
lines refer probably to the polyp and sexual medusa
stages (upturned and downturned vessel shapes) of
the coelenterates: hydra, jellyfish, obelia . . .

now the other world, this place, THIS IS . . . .
. . . .
THIS IS . . . . . . + + + + + + + + + + + + + ... + + + + + + + + +
. . . . as they are leaving me as they leave, sperm

and tears go out, and pus goes out, and piss, and they leave,
everything's always going out, they . . . .
. . . . pattern (shoes?) for the [Sheol] of Pinitou
. . . . out like sweat, like earwax, like shit, nothing + + + + + + + + +
+ + + + + + + + + + + + + + + + + foxglove . . . . holds
his long man . . . . this unexpected place THIS IS . . . .
hurtling turnaround lightthring paws ship cockshead alone for a toy
I walk when I walk

        when I walk I walk

                I walk when I walk, they . . . .
they follow they afflict they follow THIS . . . .
. . . .
. . . . loveliness

in the face of a bog	with jealousy
in the face of a creek	with jealousy
in the face of sometimes-wet-hard-thing*	with jealousy
in the ear of the last shallow breath	with jealousy
in the face of salad greens	with jealousy
in the guilt of clay ear-plugs	with jealousy
in the eyes of swell-shrink*	with jealousy
in the face of thin-thin-fat*	with jealousy
in the life of the round dance	with jealousy

                    * approximations. Cognate fragments suggest that the
                    reader may continue the list ad lib, with group re-
                    sponse continuing.

when I walk, I walk, I must say I walk when I walk
I have that I have had that
no envy of Old No-Name gets to me I have these legs of laughter
everything always keeps leaving me, it is
never enough, I've surrendered the damp lips of speech
emptied these eye sockets, filled my ears with good clay, ground down
my fingertips I'm left like a dog to smell my way to the dream
THIS IS AN EMPTYING. so much living . . . . forgiven
. . . . + + + + + + + + + + + + + +
. . . . in the face of a creek reeds come back
+ +

TABLET X

.... + + + + + + + + + + + + + +
+ +
+ + + + + + + + + + + + + + + +
+ + + + + + + + + + + + + + + +
+ + + + + + + + + + + + + + + +
+ + + ... ⊕ ⊕ ⊕ ⊕ ⊕ ⊕ ⊕ ⊕
.... + + + + + + + +...... + + + + + + + + + + +
+ + + + + ... + + + + + + ... + + + + + + + + + + + + + +
....
.... ⊕ ⊕ ⊕ ⊕ ⊕ ⊕ ⊕ ⊕ ⊕ ⊕ ⊕ ⊕
+ + + + + + + + + + + + + + + + + + +....... + + + + + + + + + + +
+ + + + + + + [the the] + + + + + +
+ + + + + + + + + + + + + + + + + + +
+ + + + + + + + + + + + + + + + + +
+ + + + + + + + + + + + + + + + + +
+ + + + + + ... + + + + + + ... + + + + + + ... + + + + +
....
....
....
....
....
.... + +
.... + + + + + + + + +

BLET XII

This tablet constitutes an extraordinary find, a
an even more extraordinary translation. I pres
this text with delight and a humility which ur
me to incorporate a quote into the introduction
this, the first musically notated chant in writt
human history. Many readers will recognize th
the following citation stems from that mesmerizi
work, published recently by the Press of the U
versité de Strasbourg, *The Music of the Sumeria
and their Immediate Successors the Babylonians a
Assyrians* by the Sumeromusicologist F W Galpi
Litt. D., F. L. S., Canon Emeritus of Chelmsfo
Cathedral and Hon. Freeman of the Worshipf
Company of Musicians. Canon Galpin writes:

'We must now allude to a very remarkable tabl
known as KAR 1, 4 and preserved in the Staa
liches Museum, Berlin.... This Sumerian Hym
on the Creation of Man is furnished with an A
syrian translation in the right-hand column and i
the left-hand column there are certain groups
cuneiform signs which seem to indicate the music

For the interpretation of the notation set to th
Hymn I am solely responsible: spurred by the wor
"impossible," I have tried to express this ancien
music in modern form on reasonable and acknowl
edged lines. Unfortunately we shall never mee
with anyone who was present at its first perform
ance and could vouch for its certitude. I must there
fore leave it to my friends and critics to say whethe
they do not feel that these old strains of nearly
4,000 years ago and the oldest music we have are
indeed well-wedded to the yet more ancient words.'

, what
ou have us do now?
re do you ask us for?
the question
the time of the making of a pair
rth and heaven
e time
our Mother Inanna
hen she came

TABLET XI

whenever I was open I was closed *

> * who is speaking here?

where? when you took them with him?
she opened her vagina so late it was no prophecy it was .... +
whenever I opened your vagina*

> * who is the narrator?

she was a prophecy no later drainage could make up for
and never mind the vats of fresh (urus-shit?) *

> * clearly an allusion to unusably new fertilizer; a po-
> tential scorching of the soil?

where did you take her when the vats ....

+ +

for the bloody wisent for the [spermy] (frogs?) *

> * who is speaking here?

lots of people opened that door
splayed on the butchering dust I opened my thighs
where? when you took them with him?
the island flowers the swamp flowers*

> * might this be an initial allusion to the Good Land?

she took him with them for her
where? .... with him for it?
she opened her + + + + + + + + + + + + + + + + + + + and never minded
she took him splayed from them to cover it*

> * singular confusion of pronouns here. I do not know
> who I am when I read this. How magnificent.

pressed down to raaling goruck juice by copper vats by prophecy
when you took them with him

as they were shown through the entrance she whinied like the auroch
where I . . . . and she reared
in every case they . . . .
when we . . . . all together . . . .⊕ ⊕ ⊕ ⊕ ⊕ ⊕ ⊕ ⊕ ⊕ ⊕
o and a life a life a life a life a life a life a life
a life a life a life a life a life a life a life a life a life a life a life
punctured by valleys, never even, punctured by punctures
punctured and punctured and what's left is fingernail
unburied, dangerous above ground, rotting slowly pintrpnit!
in the shadow of [fingernail] we (I?) + + + + + + + + + + + + + + + + + +
+ + + + + + + + + + + + + + lianregnif fo wodahs eht ni
stav gnimaets ekil serutcnup fo wodahs eht ni
suru rof efil a efil a efil a efil a efil a dna o*

* apparent sudden appearance for the first time in
these texts of the boustrophedon! reminiscent of the
Lemnos Stela of course—but how much later *that* was;
this one may be the *first* boustrophedon!

and cry with the force of testicles aw-aw-nib-gi-gi*

* this verbal, 'o answering answerer,' operates in the
hortatory vocative imperative, an idiosyncratic tense,
apparently a mood, but most clearly a real case. Cog-
nates in later Semitic (as for instance Square Arabic)
assure us that the term represents intonationally noth-
ing less than a scream of despair, released at high pitch
after the solemn incantation of three low notes, in
our notation perhaps C below the bar lines in the
treble clef. Specifics are hard here. Interestingly the
scream leads into the magic barter list, itself maybe a
cover for intermittently forbidden Utopian specula-
tions.

+ +
+ +
+ ·
+ +
+ +
+ +....
. . . . . . but if you do, give 17 washingstones for 1 cylinder seal in exchange
give a beginning (hair?) in exchange for a wood zag-sal * **

* zag-sal: an elev
** apparently the
for an instrument

give a mountain-size platter in exchange for a horde
give a risen millet stalk, give a giant rye in exch
give a healthy lettuce and a drinking-tube in excha

* according to Sa
sponsible 'for the
borne disease.'

give fresh yoghurt in exchange for a horde of our peo
+ + + + + + + + + + + + + + + ...
give a great netting of fish in exchange for a hunger-
give a milking-stool and a calf in exchange for a th
give a bone spoon and another bone spoon and anot

* the phrase 'in
of also meaning
discoverable in th
players.

give a drainage system for the miserable without patt

* we know that
archaic context
of transcendent
unequivocally, t
voice in recorde
cries out in earl
doubt that the f
mask for the wr
temporary of m
will necessary fo
most total thoug

+ + + + + + + + + + + lianregnif fo wodahs eht
stav gnimaets ekil serutcnup fo wodahs eht ni
nam rof efil a efil a efil a efil a efil a dna*

* boustrophedon
valor, we are in
is a mere 5,000 y

and nov
would y
what m
that wa
a
e
and at t
o
w

TA

                              —so it went
when earth was laid in its place
and heaven fitted
when straight-line stream and canal ran
when Tigris filled the bed
and Euphrates filled the bed
the god An
                    and Enlil the god
                                      and Utu the god
                                                        and the god Enki

sat in a high place
and alongside them
the gods Anunnaki of the earth
                              —so it went
and now
what would you have us do now?
what more do you ask us for?
said the god An
                    and Enlil the god
                                      and Utu the god
                                                        and the god Enki

what?
we've fixed earth in place
and fitted heaven
the stream runs and the canal runs
Tigris floods and Euphrates rolls
each held in a bed
can we do more?
                          —so it went
what's left, what
for us to make?
you gods Anunnaki of the earth
what do you want, what more
can you now ask us for?
the two Anunnaki gods of the earth
and wielders of fate
had a thing to say to the great Enlil:

                    earth and heaven meet, they say,
        at the high place Uzuma
        in that high place kill
        the craftsman-gods, both of them
        and from their blood
        make a man and more men

        ud an-ki-ta tab-gi-na til-a-ta-eš-a
        Dingir ama Dingir Inanna-ge e-ne ba-si-sig-e-ne
        ud ki-ga-ga-e-de ki-du-du-a-ta
        ud giš-ḫa-ḫar-an-ki-a mûn-gi-na-eš-a-ba
        e pa-ri šu-si-sa ga-ga-e-de
        id idigna id buranin gu-ne-ne gar-eš-a-ba
        An Dingir En-lil Dingir Utu Dingir En-ki
        Dingir ga-gal-e-ne
        Dingir A-nun-na Dingir ga-gal-e-ne
        bar-maḫ ni-te mûn-ki-dur-mu-a
        ni-te-an-i šu-mi-nîb-gi-gi
        ud giš-ḫa-ḫar an-ki-a mûn-gi-na-eš-a-ba
        e pa šu-si-sa ga-ga-e-de
        id idigna id buranin
        gu-ne-ne gar-eš-a-ba
        a-nâm ḫên-bal-en-zên
        a-nâm ḫên-dim-en-zên
        Dingir A-nun-na Dingir ga-gal-e-ne
        a-nâm ḫên-bal-en-zên
        a-nâm ḫên-dim-en-zên
        Dingir ga-gal-e-ne mûn-sug-gi-eš-a
        Dingir A-nun-na Dingir nam-tar-ri
        min-na-ne-ne Dingir En-lil-ra mûn-na-nîb-gi-gi
        uzu-mu-a-ki dur-an-ki-ge
        Dingir nagar Dingir nagar im-mân-tag-en-zên
        mu-mud-e-ne nam-lu-galu mu-mu-e-de

an-ki-a mûn- gi-na-eš- a-ba e pa šu-si-sa ga-ga e- de id

i- dig- na id bu-ra-nun gu-ne-ne gar- eš- a- ba a- nam

ḫên-bal-en-zên a-nam ḫên-dim-en-en-zên Din-gir a-nun-na Din-gir ga- gal- e- ne

a-nam ḫên-bal-en-zên a-nam ḫen-dim-en-zên Din-gir ga- gal- e- ne

mûn-sug-gi-eš-a Din-gir A-nun-na Din-gir nam-tar-ri min- na- ne- ne

Din-gir En-lil mûn- na- nib- gi- gi u zu- mu- a- ki dur- an- ki- ge

Din-gir na-gar Din-gir na-gar im- mâg- tag- en- zên

mu- mud- e- ne nam- lu- gal- u mu- mu- ed- e

DESIGN
TABLET

This design-tablet might actually belong in the second great section of these works, *The Filling,* or *The Holy Giving of the Self*. But I'm not sure, and feel to place it here. I have almost no indications for dating or appropriate placement: I will not number it. Its make-up and symbolic overtones, its abstractive quality and its idiosyncratic subjectivity all impel me to intercalate it here between *Tablets XII* and *XIII*.

This design-tablet is repository of secret guides for the unfolding of visionary images. Whether the meanings are functions of its functioning, or whether they are its essentiality I don't know; I do know that my long experience with it warrants that concentrated meditation in it bears metaphysical rewards of a high order.

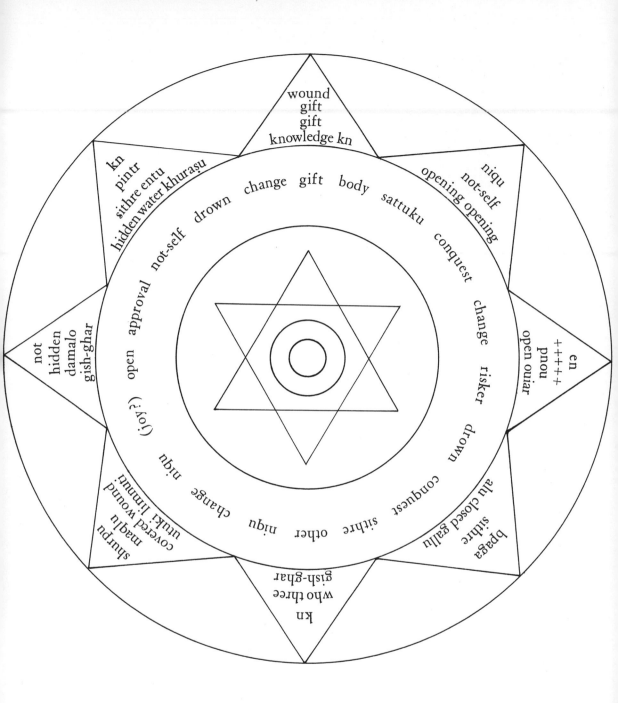

TABLET XIII

this chair this yellow table these pots this tablet-clay this lettuce this lettuce
this stone jar these blue flowers this silver lioness this electrum ass on her rein-ring
here's my eye and here's the great emptiness surrounding the object hating me
this tablet-clay hating me separated from its name
this stone jar hating me separated from its name outlining
a piece of the air to sliver me through this piece of blue flower hating me
surrounding myself in anger with me in anger with me copper adzes
hating me the white-green light around the scribe the market-pile the lettuce
hating me in a white-green light separated from its name to sliver me with ice*

> * psychotic rant; what surprises however involves the
> degree of non-analogic type of reasoning, atypical per-
> sonally and culturally, of the thought-modes of archaic
> literatures, Sumerian, Hebrew, Ugarit etc. But the
> author of XIII was very likely a "cured" schizophrenic
> looking back, intensely directed to assess her past.

when I was four the liver said you will choke you will puke out your heart
o and your life your life your life in the pit of your thinking stomach
and your feet caught in the swampy muck by the knom and your son
separated from his name hating you
let it come down said the star Nergal *

> * sun-god of midsummer, bringer of pestilence and
> death.

. . . .+ +
in the nightmare of the liver-lobes I used to read the face of Lak
from the back of a burnished brass mirror saying walk-death
. . . . gall-bladder and daylong white-green trance
in the bloody fresh sheep gall-ducts surrounding me and my balls were cut
who do you know who threes? who do you know who threes? and let it come down
the young lettuce is separated from its name and grows dwarf
the blind light surrounds the heron flying in a form
to augur the end of my name ouiar arggheyou ouiar sharmareser ouiar yorgh*

* these transliterated sounds either did or did not mean
something. The phonemic structure confuses. The re-
gressed ego cries.

underneath bronze not bronze
chameleon changes to green
no-life chameleon no change
saying walk-death
+ + + + + + + + + +
tablet tablet how do you go
I don't know
. . . .
the penis is offering
I walk under water
sharmareser yorgh
last year I had a woman
open to the rain and flood
or else a man with breasts
shining in a brass light in a room
I walk under water
+ + + + + + + + + + +
who do you know who threes
and grows dwarf?
come down or come down
if you gave me sour milk
sharmareser yorgh
begin begin begin begin begin begin begin begin begin begin begin begin
the voyage with quick-food *

* ambiguity: quick to digest? to nourish? or perhaps
the sacred mushroom, amanita muscaria, which like
all mycelial productions seems to sprout suddenly, like
magic, from the subsoil.

begin to begin
give the eye to the socket
surround the nostrils with the nose
encircle the cave of the mouth with lips
and the asshole with fat cheeks
the mantis eats her lover after all is done

neck first let it come down but begin

begin to begin

jar name table name lettuce object tablet-clay name

name name

eye mouth eye nostril lip cave ass tablet-clay mouth name

take light wash away light together eye nose face name name

+ (43 lines) *

* this entire section a distillation of great complexity: in this sequence of aphasic agrammatism—inability to construct proper word sequences—(described most clearly by Goldstein, the great modern student of aphasia) the 'cured' schizophrenic writer of this Tablet tries with anguished efforts to reconstitute the world of 'reality' and her place in it. These curious lines may embody the aphasic effort to find words for many familiar things by making lists. The introductory mention of the 'quick' food further suggests some possible religious context involving healing and the inward trip.

TABLET XIV

from nothing, from nothing, the stone beginning, tell me my name,
when I write letters and do accounts I am that other man
and keep from trembling, o at the heart's root is not cauldron but . . . .
come in come in come in come in says my pain
run from the sun, wander around in me and profit, the stars tell North
but little else.
               From nothing from nothing find me my name, say
in some clear way if the end is sadness, how the days of fishing are numbered, say
whether my name begins in rage or music rooting about for its pleasure
o draw me from my Alabaster Self
my millstone quartz marl me take me from my smooth whiteness my absence
o Oualbpaga Dammara Damalo Karhenmou Amagaaa Arigaaa Adambpaga
as a night lightens in dream rivers.
+ +
where does the hunger grow? never never ever
in the lines of force stowed motionless in my thighs and afloat in the mineral roe
of ground o let my secret name Dammara Damalo Karhenmou implode and boil
in my balls frozen in my body's boat
                        Oualbpaga I see the green-winged teal fly by
come in to nothing says my pain, as a mindless shoat that roots about like play.
slipping out. slipped. slobber. coast. waste. worn. envelope goat tripe. explode. opal.
nie. wye. dipple sty. Alabaster pie. armor my. spider clam close stone.
try to die. come in come in come in come in.
                        Oualbpaga I see the green-winged teal fly by
. . . .
. . . .
siren me a road father. try to die, envelope goat tripe. explode, coast pie, go below.
is it above? bebove, love. slipping out, worn zone. open clopen. daimon daddy
me me a road, me me a road myself my name Dammara Damalo Karhenmou, say
in some clear way, I say, says, it says, saying, we saying, say, say, said,
will have had, would might will will will, but find will, find blunder on, shoat roots
    about
if the end is sadness, how the days of fishing are numbered, say saying I said

begins in rage or music rooting about for pleasure it must be possible
says my pain, as a night lightens in dream rivers. hunger the hunger. say is.
. . . .
. . . .

TABLET XV

Probably the song of a temple prostitute, priestess of the second caste.

much, heavily flying, much, heavily flying, much, the vagina musk bleeding
they bring in the wild ass
slow spectrum enormity penis enormity ravage till
much, spectrum, soil-tiller, heavily flying and till till vagina musk
they bring in the wild ass
never of when whenever coming coming coming now power ziggurat tureen
of much, heavily flying, enormity ravage penis in sperm mass blue river god
they bring in . . . .
lapis and obsidian and bronze gird about gird about bronze testicles
he climbs suspension my back raw inside lips suspension my teeth together wild god
nettles nettles sacred bath of sperm and blood bronze in my sleep
+ +
+ +
+ +
for you, that I turn for you, that I slowly turn for you, high priestess
that you do my body in oil, in glycerin, that you do me, that you slowly do me
that you do me slowly almost not at all, that you are my mouth
that I am your vulva, feather, feather, and discover for you—
let me open my thighs for your hands as I do for my own that I do you
that my hair thinks of you and remembers you, that my fingers
that the sweat on my thighs/bronze bronze heavily flying/thinks of you
and reminds me of me and that you let me be harsh
o for you, that I turn for you, that I slowly turn for you, high priestess
that you do my body in oil, in glycerin, that you do me, that you slowly do me
that you do me slowly almost not at all, that you are—
+ +
. . . . that my body become a sentence that never stops, driving through air spaces
from one tablet to another, its python power
. . . . unclear, it must be the tips of my own fingers on my cunt lips
and your hands which graze my nipples, looking for what they need,
which endear the field of my closed eyes my closed eyes my nose the corridor
of my ear, my clitoris, and your wayfaring hands bearing through myself images

that constantly just escape me because I will not let them win over you,
your hands which graze my field, sentence
and inflection of how I do me, you do me and how do I how wonderful
by way of pictures I can't see thrust across the air between us high priestess
and dare to put your own hands on your own lips
my hands on yours, how is it I never knew
this took so much risking, that I do you, that you turn for me
that you slowly turn for me, that I do your body in oil, in glycerin,
that I do you, that I do you slowly almost not at all
+ +
. . . . in this small clearing where I rest from us, space inside the field,
emptied of muscle and cries, emptied
of muscle and cries my closed eyes empty cups of rest
in which your picture sometimes appalls and that you know to leave me here
where my money my clothes my blood my liver are violently plucked away from me
my field sometimes in such pain from thousands of tiny openings
and I wake up unpeopled and startled at such happiness

This book was set on the linotype in Granjon.
The display face is Sistina.
It was designed by Jacqueline Schuman,
composed by H. Wolff Book Manufacturing Co.,
and printed by Noble Offset Printers, Inc.